Fairies
And
Fireflies

Bedtime Stories

Becca Price

Wyrm Tales Press
Whitmore Lake, MI

Contents

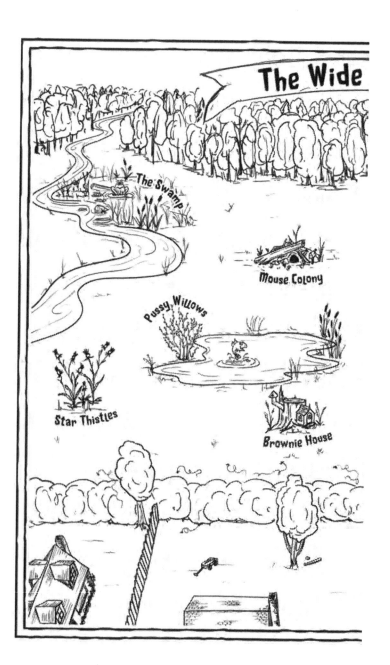

The Wide

The Swamp

Mouse Colony

Pussy Willows

Star Thistles

Brownie House

Author's Note

Dear Cassie:

When you first read "Sunflower," you asked whether Butterfly Fairy ever got her pussy willow kitten, so I wrote the story "Willow." When you beta read that for me, you asked, "is that all?" and so the story "Firefly" came about. After that, Butterfly Fairy took over and she started to tell me more stories about her adventures and her friends.

The book you hold in your hands is the result. I hope you enjoy these stories as much as you did the original "Sunflower" and the other stories in **Dragons and Dreams**.

Fondly,

Becca

Sunflower

Author's note: A version of this story also appeared in the book Dragons and Dreams.

Once, a small Butterfly Fairy flew over a patch of golden sunflowers growing in a wide wild field. Butterfly Fairy loved the sunflowers. She loved their bright orange petals and the way that the flowers always turned their heads so that they always faced the sun.

They even looked like the sun, she thought, with their

flat round seed heads surrounded by orange and yellow petals that looked like the rays of the sun.

The sun was warm on her green and purple wings, and the sky was clear and blue. Butterfly Fairy should have been very happy, but she was sad and lonely. She wanted a pet to play with, to cuddle with, to love and to hold.

Butterfly Fairy landed on the largest sunflower. She opened a pouch that hung from her belt and took a pinch of magic then sprinkled it on the sunflower. "I wish I had a kitten to play with! A soft, furry kitten to love and hug and cuddle and play with!" she said. Then she took a whole handful of magic and sprinkled it on the sunflower. "I do wish I had a kitten!"

She sat on the sunflower for awhile, but nothing happened. Soon the air grew cool and the sun began to set. Still nothing happened. Sadly, Butterfly Fairy flew home.

All that night the magic sank into the sunflower. Early in the morning, just at dawn, it began to rain lightly. The dawning rays of the sun touched the mist and a beautiful rainbow arched through the sky and touched the sunflower.

When the rainbow touched the magic in the sunflower, it began to change. It twisted and shimmered–and disappeared!

When the rain had cleared, Butterfly Fairy flew back across the wide wild field to visit her sunflowers and to wish for a kitten of her very own. But when she got there her favorite sunflower, the biggest one of all, was missing.

On the ground, where the sunflower had been, slept a soft kitten. Her fur was golden as the sun, with orange stripes like sunflower petals. And her eyes were green and purple, like Butterfly Fairy's wings. And, where the rainbow had touched her was a beautiful rainbow-colored heart.

Butterfly Fairy was so very happy! She flew down for a closer look.

It was a beautiful kitten, the most beautiful kitten she had ever seen. Her fur was as soft as Butterfly Fairy could wish it to be. But, oh my! What happened?

Something went wrong. Horribly terribly wrong! The kitten was HUGE.

Butterfly Fairy had used too much magic for her wish and had chosen the biggest flower in all the wide wild field. No wonder the Sunflower Kitten was so BIG.

The Sunflower Kitten was so big that Butterfly Fairy could sit on her head and ride between the kitten's ears. The kitten's eyes were as big as Butterfly Fairy's wings. The poor Butterfly Fairy couldn't pick up this kitten to cuddle her; if she wasn't careful, the kitten could eat her in one gulp!

Then the Sunflower Kitten opened her green and purple eyes, looked at Butterfly Fairy, and purred. Butterfly Fairy curled up by the kitten's face and stroked and petted her gigantic new friend.

Then she sat on the Sunflower Kitten's head and whispered directions in her ear. The two of them traveled through the wide wild field, laughing and playing. When they were thirsty, Butterfly Fairy drank from dew drops while Sunflower Kitten lapped from a clear stream. When they were hungry, Butterfly Fairy nibbled on a berry while the Sunflower Kitten raised her face and fed on the sun's warm light. Sunflower Kitten may look like a normal kitten, but there was still much of the sunflower nature about her so she fed on the sunlight the way other flowers get fed from the sun.

Sunflower Kitten loved to chase wind-blown leaves or tease small animals, but her claws were soft and smooth like a sunflower seed so she did them no harm.

All too soon, it seemed, the wonderful day ended and it was time for Butterfly Fairy to return home. The two tired friends traveled to her home.

Sunflower Kitten was much too big to fit in Butterfly Fairy's home, so all that night they curled up safe and warm at the base of the Butterfly Fairy's tree while the kitten purred them both to sleep.

The next morning the two friends went out again, exploring farther from home than Butterfly Fairy had ever been. They left behind the wide wild field and came near houses and farms. They were very careful that no one saw them, which was not so easy for a large yellow and orange Sunflower Kitten.

Then they saw one house all surrounded by fields and trees, with no other houses near. They heard bird songs and the rustle of the wind in the trees, but they also heard something they had never heard before. It sounded like someone crying.

On the porch of the house sat a little girl with her head buried in her arms. She was very sad because she was lonely and had no one to play with.

Butterfly Fairy and the Sunflower Kitten crept nearer and nearer. The kitten purred to Butterfly Fairy, "I'm too big to live in your home, but this house is bigger. And I love you, but this little girl needs me, too."

And Butterfly Fairy said "Yes. And we can still play together when she is busy with other things."

So the Sunflower Kitten crept closer and closer to the little girl. The girl didn't see Sunflower Kitten and Butterfly Fairy, since she was crying with her head in her arms. Butterfly Fairy flew to the girl's hair and pulled as hard as she could, but Butterfly Fairy was so tiny that the girl didn't feel it. Butterfly Fairy shouted in the girl's ears, but the girl couldn't hear it.

Finally, Butterfly Fairy whispered in the girl's ear, "Sorry," and bit the girl's finger as hard as she could. The girl felt that and looked up. There, sitting in front of her, was a yellow kitten with purple and green eyes and orange stripes like sunflower petals. The Sunflower Kitten purred.

The little girl wiped away her tears and picked up the kitten, who was almost too big for the girl to hold. But the Sunflower Kitten was soft and squishy and the little girl hugged and hugged her while the Sunflower Kitten purred and purred.

"Will you be my friend?" The little girl asked and laughed when the Sunflower Kitten patted her face with

one gentle paw. And so the Sunflower Kitten came to live at the little girl's house.

Butterfly Fairy often came to visit and to play with them. And early the next spring Butterfly Fairy found a pussy willow tree and wished for another kitten. But this time she used only a tiny pinch of magic on the soft gray flower.

Pussy Willow

It was early spring—still almost winter. Butterfly Fairy was curled up safe and warm in her little house in the wide wild field. Normally, Butterfly Fairy loved the winter time. She loved the sparkly snowflakes and how clean and white everything looked after fresh snow had fallen. She loved the bright red flash of a brilliant cardinal as it flew past the dark green evergreens. But this spring Butterfly Fairy was sad and lonely. She had no one to play with. Butterfly Fairy remembered the giant Sunflower Kitten she had made with her magic the previous summer and the fun adventures they had shared together. But Sunflower Kitten was much too big to live in Butterfly Fairy's little house and had found a young girl in the Land of the Big People to live with and to play with and to love. Butterfly Fairy wanted a little kitten to share her house and to play with.

One bright sunny day, when it was still very cold outside and there was snow on the ground, Butterfly Fairy risked going outside on such a cold day. She flew to a marshy area near a small pond. It was so windy and cold that her fingers, and toes, and the tips of her green and purple wings tingled. It was hard for her to fly into the wind; Butterfly Fairy was only a little Butterfly Fairy, after all. The wind was cold and fierce and Butterfly Fairy had to fight against it with all her strength. The cold wind frightened Butterfly Fairy, but she pushed on. Her desire for a little kitten to call her own was greater than her fears. Panting and out of breath, she finally made it to the edge of the pond where she curled up under a dry leaf to get out of the wind and to try to warm up.

Butterfly Fairy knew what she was looking for, though, and the group of trees and bushes she wanted were across the pond from her leaf. She would have to fly all the way across the pond to get there. She thought that if she flew very low across the water, maybe the wind wouldn't be as strong and she would be able to fly more easily.

Butterfly Fairy took a deep breath and then stepped out from under her leaf. The sun was warm on her green and purple wings as she stood out of the wind. There was still ice on the edges of the pond, but most of the ice had melted from the center of the pond and the water looked very cold and dark.

She took another deep breath and launched herself over the pond. She flew low over the water, where the wind was less.

She was halfway across the pond when a huge fish leapt up to try to catch and eat her. Butterfly Fairy's heart beat faster, it felt like she couldn't breathe, she was so afraid. Her green and purple wings beat as hard as they could in order to fly up and away from the fish. The fish missed her–just barely–and splashed back down into the cold water. Butterfly Fairy got soaking

wet. The wind picked her up and tossed her around over the surface of the pond. For a moment she was afraid that the wind would hurl her into the water and if her wings got wet, they would be too heavy and she wouldn't be able to fly.

The wind carried Butterfly Fairy, tossing and twirling like a blown leaf, across the pond. She landed with a plop right in the bushes that she had been aiming at in the first place. Dizzily, Butterfly Fairy picked herself up and shook herself. She was damp and cold, but she was safe and where she needed to be.

The trees and bushes grew thickly around the pond. Bright red cardinals and noisy black and white chickadees filled the branches of the trees, looking for seeds and berries left over from the previous fall. But best of all, growing right at the pond's edge, was a pussy willow bush.

The pussy willow bush had no leaves yet; it was still much too early in the spring for that, but it was covered with silver-gray catkins, little pods of soft gray fluff that were the flowers on the pussy willow tree. Some were very small, just coming out of their hard brown shells, but others were fully out: large and furry.

Butterfly Fairy was delighted. So many different catkins, it was hard to choose just the right one. She flew from one to another, measuring them with her arms. She wasn't going to make a mistake again like she did with the Sunflower Kitten and get something too large or too small to be cuddled properly.

At last Butterfly Fairy found what seemed the perfect catkin, just the right size to fit in her arms. She pulled and she tugged, trying to free it from its branch. Finally Butterfly Fairy braced herself on the branch, gave a strong yank, and the little catkin broke free. Butterfly Fairy fell off the branch, but caught herself before she hit the ground. She never let go of the silver-gray catkin.

Butterfly Fairy landed at the base of the pussy willow bush, holding tightly to her prize. Now she had to fly back across the dangerous pond and somehow make it safely to her home. She looked at the pond in dismay as the wind made wavelets across the surface. The hungry fish rose and splashed back down again, looking for food.

Butterfly Fairy was weary and worn down from her battles with the wind, the fish, and picking the catkin. However would she get her precious catkin back to her home?

She looked up at the noisy birds that filled the bushes and had a sudden idea. The chickadees weren't very bright and tended to travel in flocks. But maybe one of the cardinals would help? Or would the cardinal want to eat her like the fish had tried to do? She watched the cardinals eating the seeds and hoped that because they ate seeds they wouldn't be interested in eating a little Butterfly Fairy.

She flew up into the bushes, still holding her precious catkin, and approached one of the biggest, reddest cardinals. She stood a little distance away from the cardinal, ready to fly away as quickly as she could, in case the cardinal tried to eat her.

"Cardinal, can you help me? I need to get across the pond to my home and I'm afraid of the wind and the fish that live in the pond." she said.

"Climb on," said the cardinal. "You're so small, I can carry you all the way to your home."

So Butterfly Fairy climbed onto the back of the cardinal and cuddled down into his warm, soft feathers. Together they flew across the dangerous pond and all the way back to the wide wild field where she made her home.

"Thank you so much!" she said to the cardinal. Then he flew off again in search of more seeds to eat.

Butterfly Fairy ran into her house and put the catkin down in front of her fireplace. Then she ran to get the small bag of magic from her chest at the foot of her bed. She took a pinch of magic out of the bag, sprinkled it on the catkin, and said, "I wish for a kitten to play with and to love."

Nothing happened, but, after her experiences with the Sunflower Kitten, the Butterfly Fairy had learned that this kind of magic took time to work. Still, she couldn't resist adding another pinch of magic to the catkin and exclaiming, "I *do* wish for a kitten!" Since she was tired after her adventures of the day, she crawled into bed and slept soundly.

All night the firelight shimmered on the silvery-gray catkin. Slowly, it seemed to stretch and to grow. First, a tiny head appeared with two eyes bright as the firelight and a tiny pink nose. Then the catkin rolled over and four paws appeared, with brown claws like the shells that held the catkins to the branches of the pussy willow tree.

Very early the next morning, Butterfly Fairy awoke to find something curled up by her head and heard a low rumbling sound. She opened her eyes cautiously to find a silvery-gray kitten sleeping next to her. The rumbling sound was the kitten purring.

Butterfly Fairy was so excited. She curled her arms around the kitten, who nestled in closer. "Oh, what fun we'll have together, kitten. I'm going to name you Willow." The pussy willow kitten just licked Butterfly Fairy's hand with her rough pink tongue and purred.

Firefly

Butterfly Fairy stretched her green and purple wings in the bright summer sun. She loved to play out in the wide wild field near her home, dancing on the light breezes and the flowers that grew everywhere in the field. Even more she loved to play with Willow, her kitten that she had magicked from a pussy willow catkin. Willow was curious about everything. She liked to paw at the grass leaves that nodded in the wind with her blunt brown claws. She liked to follow the ants as they went about their busy way. She would sniff at them, and bounce away from them, pretending to be scared of them. Butterfly Fairy would laugh at her kitten's funny games. The ants ignored Willow; they knew she wouldn't hurt them and they were busy going about their work.

At the end of each day, tired from playing, Butterfly Fairy and Willow would go back to Butterfly Fairy's house in the wide wild field. Willow would curl up in

Butterfly Fairy's lap and purr while Butterfly Fairy would read if there was still daylight. Or sometimes she would just sit and pet her pussy willow kitten. They were happy just to be together.

One day, Butterfly Fairy and Willow stayed out later than usual. Twilight fell and the sky was a deep rich blue as one by one the brightest of the stars came out. Butterfly Fairy knew that they would have to return to her house in the dark. There were frightening things that filled the night, like bats that liked to eat insects, and they might enjoy to snack on a little Butterfly Fairy. In the trees that marked the edge of the wide wild field, bright green spots of light started to flicker on and off and looked as though they were dancing as they moved around.

Butterfly Fairy wanted to return to her house, but the flickering lights fascinated Willow. She started to creep toward the lights. It was so dark that Butterfly Fairy couldn't see Willow any more. She called, and called, but Willow didn't come running to Butterfly

Fairy as usual. Finally, Butterfly Fairy had to return to her house all alone. She was very sad to have lost her kitten, but hoped that Willow would be able to find her way home by the morning. Butterfly Fairy hoped that none of the scary night things would want to eat a playful, curious pussy willow kitten.

In the meantime, Willow reached the edge of the woods. She watched the lights dance among the leaves

of the trees. One of the little lights was smaller and lower to the ground than the others, and danced right up to the pussy willow kitten. It was a little firefly, an insect whose belly glowed bright green. The firefly stayed just out of Willow's reach. Willow pretended to pounce at the firefly who giggled, and danced first closer and then farther away, teasing and playing with the kitten.

Finally, the little firefly's mother called her home. Willow left her new friend and returned to her own home.

She scratched at Butterfly Fairy's door and meowed to be let in. "Where have you been, you naughty kitten?" scolded Butterfly Fairy. But she picked up Willow and cuddled her closely so the kitten knew that Butterfly Fairy wasn't really mad at her, but had been worried.

After that, every evening that Butterfly Fairy had to return to her home, Willow would go to the tall trees and play with her new friend until the firefly's mother called her in. Eventually, Butterfly Fairy got used to Willow staying out late. Willow, it seemed, could take care of herself. Butterfly Fairy would stay up at night until she heard Willow scratching at the door with her blunt claws and meowing. Then Butterfly Fairy would let Willow in and they would go to bed together.

The firefly's mother wasn't very happy about her child's new friend, however. She knew that sometimes cats liked to catch and eat insects and was afraid that Willow might try to eat the baby firefly. The mother was also afraid that Willow might scratch at the firefly and damage her wings; she didn't realize that Willow's claws were blunt and couldn't hurt anything.

Finally, the adult fireflies got together to decide what to do about this strange small kitten. They decided to make a trap to capture the kitten so that she couldn't hurt any of the fireflies. They made a little cage with twigs and grass. That night the firefly's mother kept her in and an adult firefly went to find the kitten. The adult firefly stayed just out of Willow's reach and lured her into the cage. The other fireflies closed the gate. Now Willow was trapped.

Butterfly Fairy stayed up later and later, waiting for her kitten to return home, but Willow was nowhere to be seen. Butterfly Fairy went to bed alone for the first time in a long time, finally falling asleep, worried for her kitten.

The next day, Butterfly Fairy flew all over the wide wild field, calling and calling for Willow, but there was no trace of her. Butterfly Fairy got more and more worried for her friend. Had something eaten Willow? Had she gotten lost and couldn't find her way home again? Butterfly Fairy was sad and lonely and frightened for her friendly kitten.

Day after day Butterfly Fairy searched for her kitten, but Willow was nowhere to be found.

Willow, too, was sad and lonely. She missed her Butterfly Fairy and their snug little house. At night the baby firefly would come down to Willow's cage and keep her company. Willow was comforted by the firefly's green light.

Late one day, as Butterfly Fairy was ending yet another day of searching and calling for Willow, she ventured near the tall trees. Willow finally heard Butterfly Fairy calling her name. Willow meowed and meowed as loud as she could, as if to say, "Here I am! Come rescue me!"

Butterfly Fairy heard Willow's cry. It was getting late and the bats were beginning to come out, but Butterfly Fairy couldn't leave without her kitten. She would call out Willow's name and Willow would meow back. Eventually, as it was getting very dark, Butterfly

Fairy found Willow locked in the cage. A tiny firefly perched on the cage and lit it with her glow.

Butterfly Fairy was so happy to have found her kitten that she almost cried tears of joy. But how to get

the kitten out of the cage? It was strongly built and the door seemed tightly locked shut.

The little firefly was too small to help, but Butterfly Fairy worked and worked at the grasses that tied the cage together until finally she got one knot free. If she could untie one knot, she could untie the others. The baby firefly hovered overhead, giving her light so that Butterfly Fairy could see what she was doing, and finally, Willow was free.

Willow bounced out of the cage and into Butterfly Fairy's arms. She purred and purred and licked Butterfly Fairy's face all over with her little rough tongue.

The other fireflies came down to see what was keeping the baby firefly. They were startled to see the Butterfly Fairy holding the kitten.

"Keep that cat away from my baby!" the mother firefly cried. "I don't want her to eat my child!"

"Willow is just a pussy willow catkin," explained Butterfly Fairy. "She lives on sunlight and dew and wouldn't hurt anybody. And see? Her claws are rounded and blunt and can't do any damage."

"But I've watched her pounce at my child, like she's trying to catch her." said the mother firefly. "Why would she try to catch a firefly if not to eat her?"

"Willow is just playing and I think your baby firefly is playing, too." said Butterfly Fairy. "Willow likes to play and stalk things, but she's never hurt anything, not even the ants in the wide wild field."

"We're friends!" joined in the baby firefly. "She would never hurt me, and I like playing with her!"

The adult fireflies all gathered around. They looked at Willow's blunt claws and at her soft teeth. Finally they all agreed that it should be all right for the baby firefly and the pussy willow kitten to be friends.

By now it was very dark and the bats were flying, looking for insects to eat. It was too late for Butterfly

Fairy and Willow to go home. The fireflies invited them
to stay with them in the tall trees until morning, when it
would be safe for them to go home.

Butterfly Fairy made a little nest for herself and
Willow and the baby firefly stayed with them all night to
keep them company. The three of them fell asleep
curled warm and safe in the little nest.

After that, Willow would sometimes go to the tall
trees to play with her new friend. Some nights, the baby
firefly would leave the tall trees and go back to Butterfly
Fairy's home with them. Butterfly Fairy and Willow
would curl up in Butterfly Fairy's chair and the baby
firefly would perch on the top of the chair. Butterfly
Fairy would read stories to Willow and the baby firefly
in the green firefly light.

Honey Bees

One bright sunny day, when Willow was sleeping in a warm sunbeam, Butterfly Fairy decided to go exploring. She lived in a wide wild field and there was so much to see and do that she hadn't seen half of it yet in her short life. She knew about the pond where the pussy willows grew and that it was filled with dangerous fish that would love nothing more than to eat a little butterfly-fairy. She knew about the edge of the woods where the fireflies lived and blinked their cool green lights in the dusk. She knew about the edge of the field where the Big People lived, but there were a lot of other places that she hadn't explored yet, so she decided to go see what was over beyond the wide wild field.

Butterfly Fairy flew and flew over the wide wild field until she came to the end of the wilderness. Here were trees, but not like the wild trees where the fireflies lived. These trees were neatly planted in rows, with the grass between the trees mowed low just like in the land of the Big People. Many of the trees were blooming, although some of them were beginning to have small fruits growing on their branches. It was a farmer's fruit orchard.

Butterfly Fairy was entranced by the sweet smell of the flowers and how orderly the trees seemed to grow. Big honey bees flew from flower to flower and gathered nectar and pollen to take back to their hive.

Butterfly Fairy followed the bees for a while. They were too busy to stop and play with her, though. Butterfly Fairy wondered why they were working so hard. So, when some of the bees started back to their hive, she followed them.

"It wasn't a bee hive like she had ever seen in the wild trees, but a series of boxes one on top of the other built on a low platform. The busy bees flew in with their heavy loads of nectar and pollen then flew back out again, back to the orchard.

Butterfly Fairy was very curious about what the bees did with all that nectar and pollen. She flew up close to the strange hive. There was a little space between the layers of boxes and she squeezed in between the top two boxes.

The box was filled with little six-sided wax cells that glistened in the half light of the hive. Butterfly Fairy wondered what was in the little cells. She started to walk across the top of them to check them out, but her foot went through the soft wax at the top of one of the cells. Immediately her nose was filled with the most delicious scent. She reached down into the broken cell and took out a thick golden liquid and tasted honey for the first time. She had never tasted anything so wonderful. Without thinking, she ate all the honey that was in the first cell and then broke through another one for more of the delicious honey. She ate and she ate until she was quite full and feeling a little bit sick from too much sweetness.

Then Butterfly Fairy heard an angry buzzing sound from all around her. She looked up and saw that she was completely surrounded by dozens–no,hundreds–of angry worker bees, all aiming their sharp little swords at her.

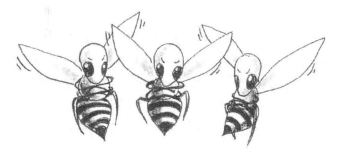

Butterfly Fairy was very frightened.

Without saying a word the bees began to close in on Butterfly Fairy.

They began to push her and shove her deeper into the hive. Poor Butterfly Fairy!

Finally, at the very center of the hive, the worker bees opened up and stopped their buzzing. There, surrounded by hundreds of drone and worker bees, was the largest bee Butterfly Fairy had ever seen. This was the queen bee, the ruler of the hive.

"Why were you stealing our honey?" asked the queen bee in a funny buzzing voice.

"I'm sorry," said Butterfly Fairy. "My foot slipped and then I got it on my hands and then it tasted so good. I didn't think."

"No, you didn't think," said the queen bee. "My workers bring the nectar and pollen from the flowers to our hive and make the honey for us to live on during the dark, cold months of winter."

"What do you do when the orchard trees stop blooming?" asked Butterfly Fairy.

"My workers will fly all over the wide wild field, looking for other flowers to find their nectar," answered the queen bee.

"I can't replace the honey that I ate," said Butterfly Fairy slowly, "but I know where the star thistles bloom and they have the most nectar of any flower I know. Maybe that will help you make more honey?"

"If you show us where the star thistles bloom," said the queen bee, "and if their nectar is as good as you tell us, then we won't sting you for eating our honey."

So Butterfly Fairy crawled out of the hive and a few of the worker bees went with her, but her hands and face were all covered with sticky honey. "Oh, dear," cried Butterfly Fairy. "I can't fly like this!"

So the bees gathered together and helped the sticky Butterfly Fairy to a small pond. "Are there fish in this pond?" asked Butterfly Fairy nervously.

"Oh, no." buzzed the worker bees. "This is a bird bath and was made to attract birds, so there are no fish in it."

At that, Butterfly Fairy climbed down from her bee ride, and splashed in the warm water of the bird bath. She had a little too much fun splashing, however, and the bees began to get impatient with her. "Show us where the star thistles grow or we'll sting you now," they buzzed.

So a rather damp (and still slightly sticky) Butterfly Fairy flew across the wide wild field, with the worker bees flying with her, to the part of the field that was covered in bright yellow star thistles. The worker bees flew from flower to flower and, indeed, the star thistles had much more nectar than any other flower they had yet found.

The worker bees flew back to their hive and danced the directions to the star thistles to the other worker bees. Many of the worker bees stayed in the orchard to fly from tree to tree, pollinating the flowers so the fruit would grow, but many others flew back to the bright yellow star thistles to gather their nectar and pollen to take back to the hive. And so the hive flourished and grew.

In the meantime, Butterfly Fairy flew back to her home. Willow was there and was happy to lick the extra honey from Butterfly Fairy's face and hands. Willow enjoyed the honey so much she purred.

Butterfly Fairy made sure not to go back to the hive again. But every once in a while, she would come home from playing in the wide wild field to find that the grateful honey bees had left her her a few cells full of the sweet star thistle honey. Butterfly Fairy and Willow would share the honey, but Butterfly Fairy was always careful not to eat so much that she would get sick.

The Littlest Firefly

In a swamp along the Big River lived thousands of fireflies. As night fell and the sky darkened, first one firefly would flash his light *blink* and then another would flash *blink* until the trees were full of bright fireflies winking their lights on and off. All of a sudden, however, the fireflies would begin to flash their lights all at the same time *BLINK* so that for just a moment the

trees would be lit up as bright as moonlight, then suddenly go dark again. The night would seem even darker when they flashed off, but then, a few seconds later, *BLINK* they would all flash on again and the tree was lit bright as moonlight again.

The littlest firefly watched in amazement. He wanted to be a part of that bright flash.

Together the fireflies lit the swamp. *BLINK* and then *blink* went the littlest firefly, just slightly off rhythm. *BLINK* they all went again and then *blink* went the littlest firefly. Try as he would, he never quite got it right.

BLINK

blink

Or sometimes he would flash too soon and go *blink* *BLINK* just a beat ahead of the others. All night long the littlest firefly tried his best to flash on when the others did, so he, too, could light the trees bright as moonlight, but he never managed it.

And so it went, night after night. *BLINK* pause *blink*, *BLINK* pause *blink*. The poor little firefly was never able to be part of that big, bright flash.

Finally, the other fireflies in the tree got together with the littlest firefly and told him, "You're ruining our display. Why don't you fly down the Big River to the next group of fireflies. They blink on a slightly different rhythm than we do and maybe you'll fit in better there."

Sadly, the littlest firefly did just that. He flew and he flew, down the Big River to the next group of trees.

That night he watched as the new colony of fireflies began their display. *BLINK* would go first one and then another, until there were hundreds of fireflies, when suddenly again they would all start to flash all at the same time. *BLINK* *BLINK* they flashed, then dark, and *BLINK* *BLINK* again. They lit their trees up bright as moonlight.

"Maybe I can do that," thought the littlest firefly. So the next time the colony of fireflies began to flash *BLINK* *BLINK*, the littlest firefly went *blink*, just off rhythm. When all the other fireflies were dark, he was the one bright tiny little light in the night between the bright flashes of the other fireflies.

"Stop! Go away," the fireflies told him. "You're ruining our display!"

Sadly, the littlest firefly stopped blinking for the night. He watched the other fireflies go *BLINK* *BLINK* pause, *BLINK* *BLINK* all night. And then next morning he continued his journey down along the Big River.

And so it went night after night. No matter the rhythm of each colony the littlest firefly tried, he could never get it right. *BLINK* they would go, bright as moonlight, *BLINK* and then *blink* went the littlest firefly.

Some colonies were harsh and cruel. When they noticed that the littlest firefly just couldn't manage to

flash in time with them, they drove him off while they batted at him with their wings until he was so sore he couldn't fly and had to rest a day or two under a leaf until he could go on to find the next colony down the Big River.

Some colonies were kind and accepted the littlest firefly. "That's all right, you can stay with us even though you don't blink at the same time as we do," they said, so the littlest firefly would stay with them for a while. Eventually though, he would get sad and leave on his own. He felt that he would never fit in.

At last, tired and weary, he came to a swamp way down the Big River. That night as usual, as it grew dark, one firefly would light up, and then another, and then another until all the trees were lit up with flashing

fireflies. All the fireflies in the tree lit their cool green fire whenever they felt like it. The lights flashed on and off randomly as the fireflies played tag and hide and seek. The littlest firefly finally found a home where he didn't have to try to time his flashes with all the others. He joined the games the others played so joyfully. When one when *blink* the little firefly would go *blink* back. So while the tree was never completely brilliantly lit, it was never completely dark either.

Urisk

Urisk was a little brownie. His parent brownies were from Scotland, but they came to the new country when their Family did. Still, they liked to follow the old traditions so they called their son Urisk, which is what they used to call brownies in Scotland.

Brownies have their favorite Families. If you leave a small bowl of sweet cream out for them at night, or a bowl of porridge, they will do jobs around the house. These were little jobs, such as fixing shoes or finishing sewing projects for you. They don't like to be thanked though. If you consider the bowl of cream left for them to be payment, they'll leave you alone. But if you leave a small bowl of cream for no particular reason, they'll drink the cream and do their work and everybody will be pleased by this arrangement.

Urisk's parents had been with one particular Family, grandfather to father to son. But when one of the Family's sons moved away, Urisk's parents wanted Urisk to go with the new Family and carry on the brownie traditions.

Urisk was still very young and a little bit small for his age, but he was willing and agreed to go with his new Family to their new home. Just to help them out. Brownies like wild spaces and Urisk made his new home in the wide wild field behind his Family's new house. Finally when everybody was settled in and it grew dark, Urisk made his way across the wide wild field. He wanted to see whether his new Family remembered to put out cream, or maybe a bit of porridge, for him to eat in their new home.

The night was very, very dark, with no moon that night. The stars were very bright, but Urisk was in a new place and was still a bit unsure of himself. There were strange noises in the night and he was a little afraid. As he walked across the wide wild field, suddenly, from the corner of his eye, Urisk saw a dark shape. He looked behind him and saw a gigantic owl flying at him.

Urisk threw himself flat on the ground and the owl's sharp talons just missed him by a hair's breadth. The talons caught in his little coat and the owl flew off,

carrying Urisk with him. Urisk struggled out of his coat and at the last minute was able to free himself and fall to the ground as the owl carried his coat away. Urisk scampered back to his little home and sat there, shivering all night long from the fright.

Night after night Urisk's new Family would leave a small bowl of cream out for their brownie, hoping that he would come. And night after night Urisk would wait until it got dark, start to set out, and became so frightened by the mere thought of the giant owl that he sat and shivered in his little home all night long until dawn. Urisk was the only brownie ever to be afraid of the dark.

One evening as it was growing dark, Urisk saw cool
green lights blinking on and off in the trees and bushes
near his Family's house. He had never seen fireflies
before. If he could only catch one, to carry in a jar with
him he wouldn't have to cross the wide wild field in the
dark. He could start to help his Family, just like
brownies were supposed to do.

The next day Urisk went out in the wide wild field
and searched for pieces of broken glass. He carefully
bound them together with his brownie magic, to create
a glass-walled cage. That night as it grew dark Urisk
silently crept out to the trees. He saw the little green
lights blinking on and off in the trees. Most of them
were way too high for him to catch, but there was one
down on the grass. It was a smaller light than the others,

but its light was bright green, and would be perfect for Urisk's purpose. Carefully, being very quiet, Urisk crept up on the little green light and when he was very close, he snatched it up and put it in the glass cage.

Urisk looked at his prisoner carefully. Up close it didn't look like much, just like any other beetle. Urisk

waited for it to start to glow and blink, but the little firefly stayed dark. Soon it was getting much too dark for Urisk's comfort and he took the glass cage home with him before it got too late.

Urisk and the firefly stared at each other through the glass of the cage.

"Well," said Urisk, "Aren't you going to glow?""

The little firefly was sullen, and silent, and dark.

Urisk carefully reached into the glass cage, so the firefly couldn't escape, and poked it.

"Go on, glow!" said Urisk.

The little firefly stayed sullen, and silent, and dark.

Urisk poked the firefly with a stick. Still no glow.

Urisk shook the glass cage in frustration. Still no glow.

"Maybe you're hungry?" asked Urisk. He wondered what fireflies ate. Since they lived in the leaves of trees and bushes, maybe they ate leaves? Early the next day, he went to the bush where he had captured the firefly and came back with a handful of leaves that he put into the glass cage with the firefly.

The firefly hid under one of the leaves and wouldn't come out.

"Maybe you're thirsty?" asked the brownie. He found a small dish, filled it with water and put it in the glass cage.

The firefly knocked it over.

"Are you lonely?" asked Urisk.

The little firefly stayed sullen, and silent, and dark.

"You know," said Urisk, talking as much to himself as to the firefly, "I'm lonely too. This is the first time I've been on my own and I can't get to my Family to take care of them because I'm afraid of the dark."

Finally, sadly, Urisk opened the glass cage and set it outside his door. "Fly away home to your family," he told the firefly. "I'm sorry I captured you."

And the firefly flew away, leaving Urisk all by himself in his little house.

That night when it grew quite dark, Urisk clenched his fists and said to himself, "This is silly. Brownies aren't afraid of the dark. I can do it. I *can* do it."

His palms were sweaty, his heart beat fast, and he felt like it was hard to breathe, but Urisk stepped out into the deep dark of the night determined to get to his Family and do his job.

Almost from nowhere there was a quiet green glow in front of him. The little firefly had come back! It settled on Urisk's shoulder and rubbed its head against Urisk's hair. If it were a cat, it would have purred.

So Urisk set out again, with the green glow of the firefly to guide him, and finally made it to his Family's

house. There by the doorstep was a little bowl of cream, just waiting for a thirsty brownie and firefly. They drank the bowl empty and then Urisk went inside the house. There he found shoes that had come unlaced and he laced them up. There was a sewing project half done on a table. Urisk took out his little needle and thread and swiftly stitched on the buttons and made button holes so finely done you could barely see the stitching. He scampered joyfully all around the house, doing all the little tasks to be done.

When he was don, he went back outside and there was the little firefly, waiting for him to guide him home. "I think I'll name you Shiny," said Urisk.

After that, every night Shiny the firefly was waiting for Urisk when he left his little house to go take care of his Family. And when he was finished with his tasks, Shiny the firefly was waiting to guide Urisk home again.

Urisk and the Fairy

Urisk the brownie set out one evening with his friend Shiny the firefly to go to his Family's house to do the little chores and tasks that he could do to help. The Family always left a bowl of cream by the doorstep for him–not as thanks, oh, no, never as thanks and definitely not as payment–no, never as payment. They left out the bowl of cream because it was a thing they had always done and Urisk visited them at night and did his little tasks because it was a thing that he had always done. This way everyone was happy.

One day, however, there was only half a bowl of cream. "Maybe a cat got at it," thought Urisk. He drank the cream and went about his nightly tasks, perhaps a bit less cheerfully than usual, but he did them and did them well.

The next night there was only half a bowl of cream again. Urisk drank the cream that was left and went about his nightly tasks, but he grumbled as he did them.

The night after that there was even less cream. Urisk drank the cream, but only did his tasks halfheartedly and left a good deal undone.

On the fourth night there was only a small bit of cream in the bowl. By now Urisk was getting hungry and rather than doing his tasks, he went into his Family's house and made mischief. Where there were shoe strings, he tangled them. Where there were dishes left in the sink, he tipped them over. He even broke a few glasses. He moved people's toothbrushes in the bathroom and left things on the floor for people to trip over. Urisk was a very unhappy brownie.

On the fifth night there was a bowl of porridge with honey left for Urisk. "Now, that's more like it," he said, but when he looked at the bowl, it was clear something had been eating his porridge with honey. "Something," he said to himself, "is eating my porridge and drinking my cream and I have to find out what it is and teach it a lesson it won't soon forget." Urisk went about his tasks again, however, because he enjoyed the porridge with honey that was left and felt that the Family had left it there to apologize for the half bowls of cream.

Just before dawn, when the night is darkest, Shiny the firefly came to light his way home again. But Urisk sent him off with thanks. He was going to spend the whole day watching his Family's house to find out who had been eating his porridge and drinking his cream.

Urisk hid himself in the bushes by the door and kept watch. He watched as one of the members of his Family came to take in the empty bowl. He watched the

children of his Family go out and play. He watched as the Family went about their business and ate their breakfast, their lunch, and their dinner. And he watched carefully as the mother of the family brought out his little bowl filled with porridge and honey and set it down carefully on the stoop. He watched as the sun began to go down and nothing disturbed the little bowl of porridge with honey.

Soon the Family began to turn out their lights and go to bed. Urisk still waited as the fireflies began to twinkle in the hedge behind the house.

Shortly after all the lights in the house were out, Urisk saw a little green light approach. Was it his firefly, come to keep him company? Or was it some strange firefly, come to eat *his* porridge with honey? He didn't think that even a whole colony of fireflies could eat that much.

To his surprise what looked like a butterfly landed on the doorstep, accompanied by another firefly that glowed to light its way. No, it wasn't a butterfly at all. It was a fairy, a little Butterfly Fairy coming to *his* porridge.

Butterfly Fairy walked up to the bowl of porridge with honey and took a dainty bite. She sighed with pleasure and took an even larger bite.

Urisk jumped out from his hiding place. "What are you doing?" he demanded. "That's *my* porridge with honey you're eating."

Butterfly Fairy was so startled she almost fell into the bowl. "Who are you?" she asked breathlessly.

Urisk had been taught good manners by his parents so he took off his little cap and said, "I'm Urisk the-wait a minute!" He slammed his cap back on his head in anger. "Never mind who I am. Who said you could eat my porridge and drink my cream?"

"Oh, is it yours?" asked Butterfly Fairy. "I didn't know whose it was. "I discovered the bowl of cream last week and thought it had been put out for a cat. I was sure the cat wouldn't mind sharing it with me."

"Does a cat live here?" asked Urisk nervously. "I didn't know the Family had a cat. I've never seen one. I hope they keep it inside."

"Don't you like cats? I have a kitten named Willow."

"How do you keep your kitten from trying to eat you?" asked Urisk. "Cats always try to chase me and eat me when I'm doing my work. That's why I always do my work at night, when the cat is asleep."

"Your work?" asked Butterfly Fairy. "What kind of work do you do?"

"I take care of my Family. They leave cream or sometimes porridge with honey out for me. I really like it when they leave the porridge; I do get a little tired of just cream all the time."

"Oh, dear," cried the Butterfly Fairy. "I didn't mean to eat your payment."

"It's not payment," Urisk scowled. "And it's not thanks. Brownies don't work for payment or thanks. It's just something they do and it's just something we do.""

"I see," said Butterfly Fairy, but she didn't, really. "Anyway, I'm sorry I ate your porridge. I've never had porridge before. It's very good, isn't it?"

"Yes," agreed Urisk, "and I'd like to eat my dinner now, please."

"Oh, certainly," said Butterfly Fairy and she backed away from the bowl of porridge, but she gave it a sad little look as she moved away.

"You can share some, if you'd like," said Urisk politely. "As I said, my name is Urisk and I'm a brownie."

"Hello, Urisk," said Butterfly Fairy. "I'm Butterfly Fairy. And thank you, I would like a little more."

Together, Urisk and Butterfly Fairy ate the bowl of porridge with honey.

"Would you like some help with your tasks?" asked Butterfly Fairy. "It's only fair, since you shared your dinner with me."

"I don't know. What can you do?" asked Urisk.

"I have a little bit of magic with me and can do a few things," said Butterfly Fairy.

"Sure, if you don't have to get home right away."

"No, my firefly will wait for me and guide me home." By this time it was very dark and the stars were coming out.

So Urisk and Butterfly Fairy crept into the house. While Urisk was untangling strings and cleaning shoes, Butterfly Fairy plumped the pillows on the couch and smoothed the fabric so that you couldn't tell anyone had ever sat on it. They both washed the coffee cups that had been left in the sink and put them in the drainer to dry. All the while they chatted with each other and were quickly good friends.

Finally it was time to leave. It was still very dark out and Urisk looked around a bit nervously. "Normally Shiny is waiting for me to guide me home," he said. "I don't know where he went since I sent him away yesterday."

"My firefly gives enough light for both of us," said Butterfly Fairy. She walked Urisk to his home in the hollow log by the pond while her firefly flew above their heads, lighting the way for them both.

"I live over by the sunflowers," said Butterfly Fairy. "You can come and visit me any time you want and play with my kitten."

"Isn't it awfully dangerous to play with a kitten?" asked Urisk.

"No, silly," laughed Butterfly Fairy. "I made Willow out of a pussy willow catkin and she's more likely to be afraid of you than to be able to hurt you. She's very tame and soft."

"Well, maybe I will come someday," said Urisk. "On days when my Family doesn't need me."

And he did.

Other Books By Becca Price

Children have always delighted in fairy tales, tales of adventure and challenge in magical lands where dragons live and The Dark is a thing to be feared and explored. From the original Grimm's fairy tales through Andrew Lang's colorful fairy books to modern classics like Robert Munsch's The Paperbag Princess, there will always be a need for, and a place for, fairy tales. My fairy tales continue the tradition with silly, serious, and poetic stories

Dragons and Dreams: Bedtime Stories

Brave princesses, grumpy dragons, princes competing for a kingdom, and children seeking answers to age-old questions. These six modern fairy tales include stories for pleasant dreams, and stories for stirring thought. They are just the right length for bedtime reading. Each is a gem that will delight the entire family.

The Snarls

The Snarls. They live on pillows and in the wind, just waiting to move into long, fine, or curly hair. And when they move in, they make nests, and more Snarls, and more nests. But we also have their natural enemies: a comb, a brush, and the dreaded Detangler spray!

This charming story makes hair combing of difficult hair not only enjoyable but a silly experience.

Child of Promise

After a summer when nothing seems to go well for a small village, the villagers are concerned that they may not survive the harsh winter. Young Agnes is chosen to go to the mountain top to seek wisdom and guidance.

This winter holiday story is not overtly religious nor sentimental, but still conveys some of the spirit of the holiday season

This story also appears in the collection Dragons and Dreams.

Quests and Fairy Queens

Quests are found in many guises, and Fairy Queens are not always what they seem. (coming soon)

Newsletter Signup

Sign up to be part of our mailing list for advance notice when new stories are due to be released. These stories include Quests and Fairy Queens, other collections, and short stories.

Please sign up at: http://eepurl.com/JA5e1

About the Author

Becca Price lives in a small town in southeastern Michigan on ten acres of weeds, swamps, and trees. She lives with her husband, two children, and three cats.

Word-of-mouth is crucial for any author to succeed. If you enjoyed this book, please consider leaving a review at Amazon, even if it's only a line or two. Tt would make all the difference and would be very much appreciated.

About the Artists

The maps are by Rob Antonishen, roba@cartocopia.com

Cover art was done by Todd Cameron Hamilton. Todd has been a professional illustrator since 1980. He has worked in a wide spectrum of media and subject matter.

Interior art is by Sara B. Anderson. Sara is a nineteen year old living in a little town on the Olympic Peninsula in Washington. There she spends her time immersing herself in all of the nature that is there. The woods, the beaches, the critters that live there, and the breathtaking mountains is where she draws the inspiration needed to create her artwork.

Dedication

To my mother, Caroline Price, who gave me a love of the mythic. To my father, Clark Price, who gave me my first Kindle, and thereby unleashed a whole new world. And to my children, David and Tori, who no longer need bedtime stories, but who I hope will always enjoy reading.

I also dedicate this to my Italian fans who are, every one of them, wonderful.

I cannot thank my beta readers enough. They have all added immeasurably to make this a better book.

32382136R00051

Made in the USA
Charleston, SC
17 August 2014